The Angel Babies 8

Dieu et Mon Droit

Clive Alando Taylor

authorHOUSE

AuthorHouse™ UK
1663 Liberty Drive
Bloomington, IN 47403 USA
www.authorhouse.co.uk
Phone: 0800.197.4150

Published by AuthorHouse 08/23/2016

ISBN: 978-1-5246-6256-1 (sc)
ISBN: 978-1-5246-6257-8 (e)

Angelus Domini .8.

I N S P I R I T * A S P I R E * E S P R I T * I N S P I R E *

Because of the things that have first become proclaimed within the spirit, and then translated in the soul, in order for the body to then become alive and responsive or to aspire, or to be inspired, if only then for the body to become a vessel, or a catalyst, or indeed an instrument of will, with which first the living spirit that gave life to it, along with the merits and the meaning of life, and the instruction and the interpretation of life, is simply to understand that the relationship between the spirit and the soul, are also the one living embodiment with which all things are one, and become connected and interwoven by creating, or causing what we can come to call, or refer to as the essence, or the cradle, or the fabric of life, which is in itself part physical and part spirit.

And so it is, that we are all brought in being, along with this primordial and spiritual birth, and along with this the presence or the origins of the spirit, which is also the fabric and the nurturer of the soul with which the body can be formed, albeit that by human standards, this act of nature however natural, can now take place through the act of procreation or consummation, and so it is with regard to this living spirit that we are also upon our natural and physical birth, given a name and a number, inasmuch that we represent, or become identified by a color, or upon our created formation and distinction of identity, we become recognized by our individuality.

But concerning the Angels, it has always been of an interest to me how their very conception, or existence, or origin from nature and imagination, could have become formed and brought into being, as overtime I have heard several stories of how with the event of the first creation of man, that upon this event, that all the Angels were made to accept and to serve in God's creation of man, and that man was permitted to give command to these Angels in the event of his life, and the trials of his life which were to be mastered, but within this godly decree and narrative, we also see that there was all but one Angel that either disagreed or disapproved with, not only the creation of man, but also with the formation of this covenant between God and man, and that all but one Angel was Satan, who was somewhat displeased with God's creation of man, and in by doing so would not succumb or show respect or demonstrate servility or humility toward man or mankind.

As overtime it was also revealed to me, that with the creation of the Angels, that it was also much to their advantage as it was to ours, for the Angels themselves to adhere to this role and to serve in the best interest of man's endeavors upon the face of the earth, as long as man himself could demonstrate and become of a will and a nature to practice his faith with a spirit, and a soul, and a body that would become attuned to a godly or godlike nature, and in by doing so, and in by believing so, that all of his needs would be met with accordingly.

And so this perspective brings me to question my own faith and ideas about the concept and the ideology of Angels, insomuch so that I needed to address and to explore my own minds revelation, and to investigate that which I was told or at least that which I thought I knew concerning the Angels along with the juxtaposition that if Satan along with those Angels opposed to serving God's creation of man, and of those that did indeed seek to serve and to favor God's creation and to meet with the merits, and the dreams, and the aspirations of man, that could indeed cause us all to be at the mercy and the subjection of an externally influential and internal spiritual struggle or spiritual warfare, not only with ourselves, but also with our primordial and spiritual identity.

And also because of our own conceptual reasoning and comprehension beyond this event, is that we almost find ourselves astonished into believing that this idea of rights over our mortal souls or being, must have begun or started long ago, or at least long before any of us were even souls inhabiting our physical bodies here as a living presence upon the face of the earth, and such is this constructed dilemma behind our beliefs or identities, or the fact that the names, or the numbers that we have all been given, or that have at least become assigned to us, is simply because of the fact that we have all been born into the physical world.

As even I in my attempts, to try to come to terms with the very idea of how nature and creation could allow so many of us to question this reason of totality, if only for me to present to you the story of the Angel Babies, if only to understand, or to restore if your faith along with mine, back into the realms of mankind and humanity, as I have also come to reflect in my own approach and understanding of this narrative between God and Satan and the Angels, that also in recognizing that they all have the power to influence and to subject us to, as well as to direct mankind and humanity, either to our best or worst possibilities, if only then to challenge our primordial spiritual origin within the confines of our own lifestyles, and practices and beliefs, as if in our own efforts and practices that we are all each and every one of us, in subjection or at least examples and products of both good and bad influences.

Which is also why that in our spiritual nature, that we often call out to these heavenly and external Angelic forces to approach us, and to heal us, and to bless us spiritually, which is, or has to be made to become a necessity, especially when there is a humane need for us to call out for the assistance, and the welfare, and the benefit of our own souls, and our own bodies to be aided or administered too, or indeed for the proper gifts to be bestowed upon us, to empower us in such a way, that we can receive guidance and make affirmations through the proper will and conduct of a satisfactory lesson learnt albeit through this practical application and understanding, if only to attain spiritual and fruitful lives.

As it is simply by recognizing that we are, or at some point or another in our lives, have always somewhat been open, or subject to the interpretations of spiritual warfare by reason of definition, in that Satan's interpretation of creation is something somewhat of contempt, in that God should do away with, or even destroy creation, but as much as Satan can only prove to tempt, or to provoke God into this reckoning, it is only simply by inadvertently influencing the concepts, or the ideologies of man, that of which whom God has also created to be creators, that man through his trials of life could also be deemed to be seen in Satan's view, that somehow God had failed in this act of creation, and that Satan who is also just an Angel, could somehow convince God of ending creation, as Satan himself cannot, nor does not possess the power to stop or to end creation, which of course is only in the hands of the creator.

And so this brings me back to the Angels, and of those that are in favor of either serving, or saving mankind from his own end and destruction, albeit that we are caught up in a primordial spiritual fight, that we are all engaged in, or by reason of definition born into, and so it is only by our choices that we ultimately pay for our sacrifice, or believe in our rights to life, inasmuch that we are all lifted up to our greatest effort or design, if we can learn to demonstrate and to accept our humanity in a way that regards and reflects our greater desire or need, to be something more than what we choose to believe is only in the hands of God the creator or indeed a spirit in the sky.

It was very much my intention not to state the name of any particular place in the script as I thought that the telling of the story of the Angel Babies is in itself about believing in who you are, and also about facing up to your fears. The Angel Babies is also set loosely in accordance with the foretelling of the Bibles Revelations.

I thought it would be best to take this approach, as the writing of the script is also about the Who, What, Where, When, How and Why scenario that we all often deal with in our ongoing existence. It would also not be fair to myself or to anyone else who has read the Angel Babies to not acknowledge this line of questioning, for instance, who are we? What are we doing here? Where did we come from? And when will our true purpose be known? And how do we fulfil our true potential to better ourselves and others, the point of which are the statements that I am also making in the Angel Babies and about Angels in particular,

Is that if we reach far into our minds we still wonder where did the Angels come from and what is their place in this world.

I know sometimes that we all wish and pray for the miracle of life to reveal itself but the answer to this mystery truly lives within us and around us, I only hope that you will find the Angel Babies an interesting narrative and exciting story as I have had in bringing it to life, after all there could be an Angel Baby being born right now.

After these things I looked and behold a door standing
open in Heaven and the first voice which I heard was like
a (Trumpet!) speaking with me saying come up here and
I will show you things which must take place after this.

Immediately I was in the spirit and behold a throne set in
Heaven and one sat on the throne and he who sat there was
like a Jasper and a Sardius Stone in appearance, And there
was a Rainbow around, In appearance like an Emerald.

Time is neither here or there, it is a time in between time as it is the beginning and yet the end of time. This is a story of the Alpha and the Omega, the first and the last and yet as we enter into this revelation, we begin to witness the birth of the Angel Babies a time of heavenly conception when dying Angels gave birth to Angelic children who were born to represent the order of the new world. The names of these Angel Babies remained unknown but they carried the Seal of their fathers written on their foreheads, and in all it totalled one hundred and forty four thousand Angels and this is the story of one of them.

~* Dieu et *Mon Droit**~

The wheels of the Ophanim began to slowly turn forth as the Archangels stood firmly in their positioning, as such was the Passover of the multitudes of innumerable and indivisible souls of the household of Selah, that upon receiving the bestowment and the blessings of the celestial Angelic Aura, that the partition began to withdraw in allowing all of those that were present and stood to watch as it opened up unto them freely to pass through.

Allowing them a passageway and the freedom to enter and to go beyond a most precious and remote place, that is held within the presence of God, for this was also the same highest realm that would be the beginning of the knowledge and the miracle for the recreation of the Earthly Heavens beyond them. Now we did all but see the face of God in his materialism, in as much that we did enjoy and experience the spirit of God that was overcoming and falling upon us all, for now what we were to do as sentient beings, except but to sit and to listen and to hear and to reflect upon God's grace within our eternal souls.

As such was the abundance of the blossoms of the auroric essences, that would allow for us to gravitate beyond our own material and bodily influences and projections, as now we did begin to learn to and to see the vision of God more clearly and with much clarity, as it was in this advancement, that we did see the Archangels break rank and fall out of file and formation, in only appearing to highlight one empty and devoid place and space, as if it had once been occupied by an Archangel of some importance, that they themselves were familiar with.

Also what was evidently present in this vast place of simple beauty amongst the stars, was the sound of quieted murmurs arising out of and emanating from the Ophanim, as if the world below and beneath us, were somehow in a state of collective consciousness, humming and breathing and whispering like a chorus of silent prayers becoming inextricably woven into the fabric of our infinite being, transcending and transmitting through the reaches of space, and yet in complete harmony with the substances of matter and that which we were now cocooned and comprised of within ourselves.

As the Archangels led us on and towards the cosmic and spiritual body of our own self fulfillment, as it was then that it became clear that the Archangel Lucifer was the missing link that had once occupied this space along with the other Archangels, and yet the dictates of time had by now proceeded along without his infinite presence, as if time itself had decided that this particular revelation within the story of the heavens was no longer relative or relevant to the dreams or further potential undertaking of tasks towards fulfilling God's graceful plan.

For the war of the words between this world and ours within this universe was now over, and yet still we had journeyed so far even beyond the limits of our own imaginings and into an unfamiliar surrounding and setting, but in knowing that we had somehow touched upon something that we had either dreamt or sought out within another lifetime, but had somehow forgotten about, except that instead we were left with the impression of something of a vested interest of something that existed long before the dreams of the Angel Babies had ever been dreamt of even conceptually realized and seen before, and yet for how long would it serve to keep us, or to sustain us in our enduring loyalty to the ophanim and throne of God.

And yet the dictates of time from the past, still reverberated with the echoes of an influential and constant reminder that was set to become consecrate and etched upon the history and finality of everything and every living being, for the time would soon begin to reveal to us, that we had already spent an eternity in the presence of all that could and ever would be, as the murmurs began to increase from their silences, and the winged creatures and of those Angels that we did not know or were familiar with, would soon begin to arise from out of their own stillness's and sleeping birth toward fulfilling their own embodiments, if only to lead us all back beyond the ophanim and towards the celestial abode and heavenly dwelling places of the Angelic Aura, and back through the Empyreans, and toward a renewed Earth, where what we had left behind, that upon our descent and return, would by now, not be so recognizable to ourselves.

Was it a renewable covenant that would serve to obstruct the past from this inevitable future, was it an unwritten contract or agreement that had passed from God's lips to ours, was it the beginning of unwritten chapter that would grant us beneath the heavens, a new Earth, with new possibilities, unheard and undreamt and unimagined, was it a final outcome upon a matter of decisive judgment of conclusive eventualities that even the least of the Archangels would be deemed to come before the throne of God, that upon our absence, and in order for all to be as it once was pronounced, a redeeming and exchangeable force of good fortunes for all concerned of our future inheritance, in that this decree would forever more remove Satan from the face of the world in all eternity and forevermore.

For the definition of the faith behind this reasoning, was that we who were to inherit this new world, would become inhibited and unable to progress if Satan were to remain in our midst, as the most influential silent proclamator of this earthly domain, and so for the face of the world to change, then so too were the influences of the world to change, and yet if this was God's beloved kingdom and earthly paradise, then why would he even allow so much disloyalty and disobedience become beset upon us, and yet favorably still display so much favoritism and further more pour out so much love, and still apply so much wisdom within his caring and compassion, and yet still maintain so much kindness and understanding to one that would instantly defy and undermine his every will. A will which could so easily smite down in an instant, for even from the origins of creation the answer to this solution was to be fortified and embedded within his namesake, for the Archangel Lucifer is the elect, and yet overtime,. Satan is the fallen, and so therefore the restorations of the Earth required that the Archangel Lucifer be restored to his origins, and yet for the betterment of this profoundly sound judgment, then equally it is for Satan to be cast out.

For it is not so simple to say that one is also the same as the other, for one is wholly obedient to the service of God, as we are all, and yet equally one is opposed and serves himself as an adversary against God, and so if we are to remove the head of the serpent as a symbolic gesture that Satan had become overpowered and removed from the Earth, then equally are we not bound to give this right over to God in reviving his most trusted and elected and most favorable of all Archangels, in that we must also learn to accept and to agree with ourselves, that even we have returned to the origins of our own heavenly birth cries and spiritual conception.

As it would be that the Archangel Lucifer's only defense in favor of Mankind, would be offset against the admittance of our very own sins, and transgressions, and our own wrongdoings and blasphemies and crimes in acting in accordance with this historical evidence as leverage towards seeking God's grace, and so therefore we are all subject within this inquisitors trial of insinuating accusations that fly across the breadth of time, giving rise to these afflictions of long suffering persecutions, that have caused us to speak and act out of error within these denials of determining detriments unfolding upon us, that in their accumulation, are now only there to serve us, as pillars of truth, that are yet to be rectified and corrected and upheld for all to see, as even we who are held in contempt as Satan attempts to destroy Humanity by casting suspicions and doubts of aspersions and causing blame to be cast upon the heads of the innocent.

For as much as this judgment is a reckoning of the past and of previous and even current deeds, then let it be known that it is also an account of adoration and respect, and humility in praiseworthy, and admiration upon the notable recognition that the Archangel Lucifer, whom is also referred to as the Bright and Morning Star, only sought to uphold and emulate God's graceful activities, which in itself could only serve to earn and be seen and recognized as exemplary in its creation, but to covet and to imitate God's own perfection through mirrored effects, is in itself to create error in defiance and disrespect and disobedience in causing separation from the whole, and bringing chaos to the order of the natural and living world, but let it also be known, that by this period of time of precreation, that the Archangel Lucifer had fallen so low in bringing about his reproaches towards God, in that this would upset the balance of the heavenly order also, in causing instability and impermanence to take effect, and so the Archangel Lucifer was by now divided from God, and only to referred to and mentioned as that old devil Satan or that serpent of old.

Now let it also be known why we the children of God are so perfectly bound up and poised in being and becoming readily able prepared for this judgment, if only to be used as pawns within the vast context of this profound and influential narrative, and that is to say that this story of the universe however significant, for whom Archangel Lucifer is also present and amongst the firstly elected along with the God of our creation, are notably also said to be of the very same origins of this universe, which upon explanation and clarity and by their very definition, primordial beings, which means to say and suggest and imply to tell us, that by this design, they are both eternal and immortal beings, whereas Satan in being cast down, is somewhat partially influential, although very much disempowered and limited in his ability to affect to God's own creation, and so we as beneficiaries of Mankind who are to inherit this Earth, are no so evenly matched and balanced of stable enough to deal with the tooing and froing of good and right, and bad and wrong actions, and so therefore, we are also in subjection to the polarities of not only the God of creation, but also we are influenced by the Archangel Lucifer, as well as the demoralized and now demoted Satan.

And so a question is posed, of whom shall it be left too, to lift up humanity up to its' rightfully and justified place of a redefined inheritance that is the Earth, as we upon all representation, and upon all investigation, and after this searching, looking and seeking and finding through our own examination of internal questioning, can now only lead us to declare and submit, that the sole answer and responsibility lies within and is left to us, as in receivership and as recipients of the Earth, that we who should not just sit around as idle laborers in our inquisitiveness, allowing for inertia to be beset upon us in the form of stagnation as immovable objects born of idol worship, for the world, even now in our absence, and also upon its; renewal and renovation, have come thus this far to uncover the truth of our history in the revelation of solving this mystery, that even now Satan is beneath us, and yet the Archangel Lucifer, is yet to be seen as redeemed and reinstated and brought back into the sights and the presence of God's good grace, and what also his fellow sentient Archangels, who hold him in corruptible contempt for his displays of disloyalty and inability to hold steadfast to his role of file, rank, and position, so that Mankind can become set upon a new and unique path of redirection towards the fulfillment of God's promises to Humanity, then so let us call for reparations to be made before we call for trials and punishments to set one child against another, and let us call for unifications and restorations before we call for condemnations upon the heads of the perpetrators of those fallen victims, and let us call for love as an example of forgiveness to those who would only assume superiority over the weak and the sick and the poor and defenseless, for is this not the truth of the nature, and the way of the future that lays the way ahead of us, for how else is God's discipline his Bright and Morning Star, his fallen elect, his discredited opponent, his foe and adversary, if we do not select and elect ourselves as ambassadors to take on this precedence and lead by the very definition of our own integral example of wisdom and understanding.

As it has been said across the ages and aeons of time that Satan cannot cast out Satan, even when is has not been said that Satan is now and forevermore cast out, which in itself calls into doubt the why and the wherefore this trial may take place, shape, and form, but if Satan is divided, then let the God of love and compassionate wisdom divide Satan from the Archangel Lucifer in order to free the world from his dominion, as we have already witnessed this new creation within this vibrant context of all modernity and innovative and progressive endeavors of monumental and momentous discovery, yes Mankind has the proven ability to excel far beyond himself, except that through Satan, man is also divided away from God's love and hope and grace towards him, for what is Mankind except the created born of the stem of the creator, and what is Satan, except a deceiver of nations and cunning deception, and yet what can we say the of Archangel Lucifer, except that God has commanded thee to now and forevermore leave this world alone from your meddlesome behavior, so that the contemptuous Satan may be extinguished and brought out of it, for you are to no avail and to no more and to no longer cause disruption and corruption in a bid to provoke God's wrath in your own conceited attempts and efforts to destroy and to deceive all nations.

For is it not better for Satan to be extracted and uprooted and disposed of in such a way so as to remove the toxicity of waste and decaying sicknesses that have plagued and infected us for an eternity, along with the pollution of illnesses that have manage to affect our physical and spiritual capabilities set as an environmental stumbling block upon the Earth from one generation to another which had led us to become fallen by the wayside in misery and despair, as this is the legacy of Satanism at its worst that stands in defiance of God, which has also brought with it disillusionment and destitution to the world, so much so that we must proclaim that this judgment must be implemented and maintained in coming to surpass the ages set before us, and in bringing about good and wise counsel in our endeavors in rectifying a renewal of our bearing and fruition of this inheritance.

As we of the world as the world in itself is also in mourning and sickness, as we in the world have become as perishable and sufferable souls in our separation away from God, for Satan has brought with himself, a great curse into the world, so much so that the Earth is dying in sickness and ill repair, as we of the world must prepare to restore the Earth back to health and vitality, as it is in need of healing and cleansing and purification, not only of itself but also of all the nations that are to be served and saved upon the declaration and passing of this judgment.

And so if it were proclaimed that Satan were to be laid so low, and then tied up, and bound up, and thrown into an abyss for a thousand years, and then released again to avenge this judgment as an arch adversary and challenger against God, for this the divine purpose of rule over the dominions of the Earth, then what of the Archangel Lucifer, for have we not seen in our historical records, that more than a thousand years in flight have already passed us by, then surely the time has come to let it be known, that the chief musician and the chief physician have already and justly, and poetically, and surgically removed the head of the serpent by expelling the scourge and the poison from the cancerous and infected wound in expelling it from the Earth, as also the song of the harp has already been sung to usher in the healing of creation, so how can we not submit to the will of God in knowing and in learning of the many ways with which it has pained God emotionally and sacrificially to contend with this, and to attentatively address this with, and to compassionately deal with this, even through the heart of tenderness born of affection, in knowing that in all of this, that God is still willing to bestow upon and pour out his undying and unending love, with patience even unto his servant, and even in chastising his beloved servant, for Satan is only the outer shell and defiled appearance of this fallen one, but as

17

for the Archangel Lucifer, for whom God is to be paid compliments and held above all, in the highest esteem of references, and adored and reflected upon with great admiration, and to be looked upon with the sincerest of attributes and adoration, and to be greeted and held dearly with the greatness of respect and affection, then what if Satan were to become no more, then what would be causes if the Archangel Lucifer would still suffice and remain to be, what then.

And so I stand before you, to declare in seeking to ask and command you, you amongst the most bountiful and of the most beautiful of Angels, you who are the Archangel Lucifer, in seeking to know what is wrong with the world and of those who dwell within it, and who has infected and poisoned God's creation and led the nations unto their own destruction, and what does it profit you to possess this world and yet lose your own soul within seeking this possession that cannot be and is not of your creation, and how will you choose to respond upon replying in earnest to the examination of these questions, for if one is described as the fallen deceitful devil serpent of old, then permit me in also asking, how can it be solved that you, who would choose to give an accurate and honest and worthy and personal account of your interfering and menacing acts of misdeeds, if one such as you is presented to be dressed as a wolf in sheep's clothing, then tell me how can the shepherd attend to his rightful flock when they know not that something sinister and is disguised now moves in and amongst them, for it is upon that submission, that you yourself shall smite the bearer and cast out upon expelling that which is your own expression in yelling, that is it Satan that has done this thing and committed this atrocity, and so it shall be upon this testimony that Satan shall be blotted out from the world at large, and upon that submission of truth if not guilt, the Archangel Lucifer shall become separated from himself and brought back into the presences of God and his Archangels.

For even unto we who have heeded the calling of the prophets and the sages and the soothsayers of the past and previous ages, in that we have understood the urgency in being ushered and urged and forced to become removed for a time from the face of the Earth, and yet in becoming absent from the world, that we in our exile and in seeking refuge upon this exodus of abandoning our future hopes and dreams and aspirations, knowing that we could not be distinguished between right or wrong, or between good amongst evil, as it was because of these tenets and acts that were committed against us in the mane of Mankind unto our Humanity, for if it were not for the errors of the dictates of Satan himself unto the world, which was by now filled with a vileness of chaos amongst confusion, and hatc amongst loathing, so how could we stand by to witness these injustices, and how could we abide to stand by and take part in participating in such a venomous revulsion against God, for was it not a bitter sweet victory, that instead of the Earth that would allow our nations to draw closer together in union and upon closing our ranks, that instead we would inherit heaven itself.

So it is upon this principal in asking and also in denoting, that how can we expect to return and to live, and to work, and to prosper, and to play in this future world, if Satan still holds it to ransom even if he is found to possessing one iota, or one token, or one gesture, or one stake upon it, then if so, then let us return to the promises of the God in pronouncing judgment upon this world in order for us to be rid of Satan, for it is folly upon ridicule, and a falsehood of mockery if Satan is permitted to translate the future and hold counsel with Governments, and present the nations with a false interpretation of false doctrines that speak no oaths of truth in favor or our representations of God.

If God is pleased with us for our loyalty to the throne of God, then let him also contend to find displeasure with Satan in leading us upon a path of futility in our corruption, for even in our yearnings and pleading and begging for love and compassion and wisdom and understanding in our perseverance of our right to equality and leadership, let it be known that Satan did all upon his appointment in fulfilling our hopes and aspirations upon this hope in our requests in seeking happiness and favor with God, so let him become disapproved and discredited and branded as a liar and a thief and a cheat in stealing our birthright and using us a bait, and placing us like pawns to ill effect and desire to turn God away from us whilst misleading Mankind unto his own Humanity towards his own downfall and destruction within the mysteries of this world.

For what of the children of the God, for what of the children of the universe, for what of the children of love, of this beloved love, for where are we going and what will become of us between the heavens and the Earth, and what of our history, and what of our legacy, and what of our future, and how will we be remembered, when we are no more than just a footprint upon the Earth, and how will we be remembered when we are no longer their salvation, and what of the time spent between the abyss and the sanctuary of this world, and what of the nations that come up our of the world in seeking answers to these unanswerable questions, and what about the rising winds and the setting of sun's, and what of tomorrow if we are to remain and yet become changed and yet still be found to be in searching and crying out, for what will content us if we are to die whilst Satan still lives, and what will nurture us when the sun dies down and nighttime besets upon us, and yet Satan still exists from one day to another, tell us who, who then shall we turn too and call upon in this world and beyond in other worlds upon this trial of destiny.

Even in the darkness of the void, there is sound, even in these words there are truths, even as the sunsets as a beacon of light, still its' rays reveal a path that leads the way, even as the moon strikes the oceans and the wind whispers in the trees, as long as I can hear you I am with you and besides you, and as much as I enduring to seek out new pastures, if only for us to take rest and refuge within the sanctity of mankind's rise to perfection, I am also rising to perfection, as it is this new heaven that shall give shelter and protection from the onslaught of elements upon the recovery and the renewal of the Earth, as all that ever was of Satan will be no more.

And so it was that the winged creatures and the other Angels that we did not know, went out before us to conquer, and to overpower, and to subdue, and to eliminate any demons that may lay in waiting thereof, in order for them to restore the Earth to in all its many fascinations and wonder and glory, as it was in their faithful preparedness of our coming forth out of heaven unto our declared prominence and in our victory of deliverance, that we should be caused and forced to move across the length and the breadth and the depths and the heights and the length and the circumference of the Earth in order to be reestablished upon it as our inhabitance.

If these are the last days, then at least let this be the last day for us to fulfill the legacies and the prophecies of old, which is also for now, for us to reconcile with all peoples of all nations, and in by doing so, then let us drive out Satan from his hiding places and restore and replace it with acts of healing and with displays of virtue and kindness, and let us also stamp out Satan's authority that has become binded up with his followers and disciples, and let us also discipline

21

them accordingly to the will of God that is forgiveness and kindness and mercy for their misguided concepts, and theories, and views, and errors of breaches in their misinterpretation of believing and trusting in a nihilistic damnation of God's creation.

For are we found to be so defenseless in calling out, and in relying upon God to meet with our every need, and whim, and distress, in order fulfill our bargaining, and yet why have we not been found wanting and needing and praying and wishing to fulfill God's needs of divine grace and purpose upon this noteworthy blessing, and yet even in addressing our own personal needs, we have carelessly forgotten and excused ourselves from pursuing and asking, what are the perfect and sustainable needs of God that we can offer unto his enduring unending, if only for us to fulfill and have it met with, and why have we not examined his wishes, as if God was in need of naught else, except that we should no less in our expectations of lavishing our praise and divine worship upon him, that all is met with and satisfied in recognition of our calling upon his holy name.

Then at least let us appeal to God, to tell us, and to inform us, and to show us, and to encourage us, and to kindle us, and to nurture us as perfect beings, so that we may be willing and able to attend to his every wish, and every need, with perfection and without cause or error, let us appeal to God to send us, and to give us a perfect example that cannot be trampled, or vanquished, or dismissed away, or ridiculed, so that we too can know how to choose wisely and correctly, in the many ways that God has fashioned us, for are we not happy in our own fulfillment and commitment when we meet with God's needs, and moreover, is not God happy with us, when he contends and meets and attends to addressing our needs, and do we not sing and dance and rejoice in jubilation when both God's needs and our needs have been addressed and evenly met, is this not the promise and the conviction of our commitment and agreement between the covenant of God and his people.

For have we not earnestly prayed, and have we not thankfully worshipped, and yet lastly and least of all, why did we not think to consider of the fruits of our labor when presented before God, if they would be properly placed and pleasing to him, even though because of our needs, and in our thirst of receiving God's love, we did not think to put God's needs before our own, for yes in agreements we have prayed for our own needs to be met with accordingly, and so therefore let us now become quiet and silent, as Selah has become quiet and silent in her own meditations, in deservedly meeting and addressing God's needs and then let us recover and engage our minds and souls as one with the true nature and purpose of God, so that the spirit of God may move within and beyond and above and across us, and therein descend upon us, if only so that our minds and souls may become blessed with the true nature and correct behavior with what God is expecting and instructing us to do to gain favor and worthiness within his sights.

For would we not turn to God if were so disadvantage and beset upon, and would we not turn to God if we were already provided for, and would we not turn to God if we were already at peaceable ends and ease with ourselves and our neighbors, and would we not turn to God if we had already achieved fulfillment and contentment, for it would appear to be that we have taken God's good graces for granted, and in by doing so, we have taken advantage of each other in our ambitions attempts to become popular, or wealthy, or successful and fruitful, for how could we neglect and set God aside in favor of materialistic and false possessions for if it were not for God, then how could it be that we would make such achievements, and so therefore even when we have achieved everything it would seem and be as though, that without God we had acquired nothing.

Are we not found to be apologetic and ashamed for our carelessness and our selfishness, even though God has be seen fit, to guide us safely by the wayside, and yet still we display such traits like the naivety of children who are yet to become mature adults, and yet what we may ask of God we could not fulfill ourselves, but instead we pray and wish for all things knowingly to come to pass, and in saying so, is God not all things to all peoples and all nations of this world, in bringing about the future to come towards and to meet us upon our journeying, and so if one is blessed, then let us all become blessed, and if one is lifted up, then let us all become lifted up, and if one is loved, then let us all become loved, as we must now all adhere to fulfill all these promises of what it is that we may ask of God to perform in our namesake.

For are we not the creation of the creator, who has come amongst us, and has administered as the Doctor, and yet who has come amongst us and has experimented as the Scientist, and yet who has come amongst us and has led us like the Leader, and yet who has come amongst us, in bearing the invention of the Innovator, and yet who has come amongst us, with the breakthrough as the Pioneers, and yet do we not now pay heed to the words of the Teacher, and the words of the Poet, and do we not now pay heed to the intellect of the Philosopher, and do we not now pay heed to gaze upon the works of the Artist, and do we not now pay heed to realize our dreams and witness the vision of the Visionaries, for if it were not a gift and a blessing born of God, then to whom else would we hold to account and to accord to have created it.

So why is it that we should turn away from one another in our despairing, and yet seek to turn to God when we are overcome by emotional tears of distress and crying out for help and attention, that surely in the Ten expressions that we would possess, that when we are found to be in prayer, that all God would ask of us, is to offer up one simple and basic expression of sincerity of invested interest unto to heaven to be heard, and yet still he would only seek to assure us, and to sustain us, and to support us, and to bless us with the Nine expressions that remained, for it is only for our safe keeping, for surely of the one expression that God would ask of us to do in his service, is to also turn to one another with such expressions, that we in turn should comply in addressing, and greeting, and fulfilling one another's wishes, to be met with the most humblest and simplest of basic needs, if only for us to greet each other with kindness, as I now turn to you, then surely you can also turn to me and those of Mankind and Humanity, so that we too can come together in supporting each other in the celebration, and in the joy and in the love of God's good graces.

For if we forget the world for one moment, then do we not remember ourselves, and yet in forgetting the world we also recall and remember God, for mankind's mind if full of untamed thoughts and wild ideas, and so therefore our minds and thoughts can wander and stray beyond ourselves, but instead we see the world and not each other, as we are separated from it and also from one another, and so therefore for humanity's sake, let us forget the world for one moment, so that we do not stray so far away from God with our untamed minds and wandering spirits and wild ideas, as for each other we have become constructed, and so let us receive one another in kindness, so that God is also pleased with us upon also receiving us with such virtues of kindness, for if we forget God for one single moment in time, then do we not face the world alone, and become as those who are without faith or love to guide us, as mankind's heart is also easily led astray and distracted by the world, and so let us remember that instrumental heart is also the true voice of God, and so let us listen to what love has to say in our faithfulness, so that we may seek to uncover and to declare our purpose in the one trueness of God.

Out of the heart arises the voice of God, for if one could see that those among us from the North, and those among us from the East, and those among us from the South, and those among us from the West, that it is upon this occasion, that we should now all be drawn together in announcing that if you believe in God, then surely there is no indifference amongst us, and yet if we say that we do not believe in God, then let the voice of the heart speak in saying, that we extend God's love and graces to you also, as there is no indifferences in and amongst us, for God does not choose to love one and not the other, for what is love amongst the faithful, except that in loving the faithless, the voice of the heart is also God, for before we choose to attempt and to decide to erect and build temples of faith to worship God, then first lest us contend to restore and resurrect the voice of the heart, which is the true voice and purpose of the temple of God.

And so why is truth so important, well it is truthful to say that truth is so important because Mankind seeks to uncover the evidence and the authenticity and the mind of ability to Verify the relevance and the proof of God, as truth is also of paramount importance concerning this matter of God, and yet we must proceed to question even how Mankind is to be explained, and we must also uncover, how we are positioned and established in becoming revealed to one another as God's creation, as much as Humanity is born to unearth and to discover and to search out, if only to detect the origins and the identity of God, if only in order for us to understand in coming and drawing nearer and closer to God, as it is noteworthy in mentioning, that to suggest and admit that Mankind has already detected and uncovered the manuscripts and the scriptures of the ages of time, written and down prepared by scholars if not early Humanitarians or historians, in claiming the verity and the proof that claim to knowingly interpret from God to his creation, his holy words of reverence, and yet we must be aware that God is more than just words alone recorded within these manuscripts and scriptures across the ages, as God is and will always be Life itself.

As from the primordial origins of time and our existence, Life is also truth, and so as to what the reality of this life determines itself to be, as it is by acknowledging so, that we must not bare false witness in the submission of our evidence that God however remote in this dimension, is and will always be a fruitful bow of abundance, even in this age of modernity, as even as we attempt to examine these manuscripts and scriptures of a bygone era, it seems that we would always come to uncover in finding, that this truth in particular, also mentions in volumes, that the suggestion of God has become influential, in that they have become collected up since time immemorial, as throughout history up until the present day, God is always and forevermore dwelling within us, even unto these modern days and beyond, for if Mankind forgets God, then he defaults in losing his own birthright, and in by doing so, he then declares this world as a false witness in saying that there is no God, and yet concerning the truth and the exact nature of God's immovable presence and subconscious spirit, which is also moving at will within and amongst us, is proof that the truth, however profound, and however unfathomable, and however distant from our own personal realities and experiences, is personified by God, and that is to say, is that God knew us much longer and much before we knew God, as even in our examples of teaching, that our mothers and fathers also knew us much before we knew them.

Even as the Earth from its' origins is also primal and yet still beyond Mankind and Humanity, then how be it that she still manages to surpass the age old influences and presences of Mankind upon the face of it, and so unto who are we to attribute to its creation, for even we in ourselves can truthfully and honestly say, that we did not create it, and yet we are the occupants and the inhabitants upon it, and in saying so that we recognize and call this world our home and inheritance and dwelling place, and yet even as Humanity in these modern times are still found to be searching, and seeking out, and looking for the primordial forces of this, our evolution of this Earth, and yet is it not now better for us to say that we do not know from how, or from when, or from whom the creation of this Earth came about and brought us into being, and yet still this is not enough to satisfy the Humanity of Mankind's tomorrow's and so on, and so therefore we are still found to be searching within our own enquiries, and still we are learning in our examinations of it, and still we are growing with understanding within our comprehending of being in subjection to this greatness as mere children of the universe still in our infancy, and yet still we have managed and found it, that even in our own pursuits to also become like the creator, if only also to create and to bring forth from out of the subconscious depths of our own imaginings and minds ability to surpass and overcome the most extraordinary of feats, that reconstruct the building blocks that constitute life, and so what is God if not the creator unto the created of creation.

Even as we speak and observe in this debate and upon this hearing, as foretold and aforementioned of the future of the world at large, in that she is now embedded like a precious stone amongst the stars of this material universe, then we must also see clearly, that Mankind has already found the means and even the capabilities to destroy if not the Earth then himself upon this reckoning, as even the peacekeepers of this fertile and yet harvested Earth, have also been met with futile struggle within their means of diplomacy, and yet trying tactics of appeasement and yet less than prevailing attempts to resolve all world wars, if only for Mankind to reconciliate with all nations of Humanity unto the practical ways of peace, and yet if Mankind sees himself as God, then is not this inevitability forecast to bring about the immensity and imminence of war across the ages, and yet if Mankind also has holds within his grasp the instruments of power over life and death,, in possessing who shall live and who shall die, then is not Mankind in defiance of his own Humanity, and yet if Mankind decides within himself as to whom he shall dictate too, as to who shall live and who shall die, then is he not guilty of the contemptible notion and propagation in this defiance of that also which results in bringing about all the nations of Humanity unto war, and for them to come into contention with one another, if only to reap the futility of war as orchestrated by the warmongers, as even with those who have become opposed to God, haven't they also declared war on heaven, and yet those who are found to be amongst us as the voices of reasoning opposition, haven't they also misled Humanity with their doctrines in their dissent in saying that God has favorably selected one race or nation over or above another, is this not the error of the way and justifiably so, that this is not found to be prove worthy in itself, as this is not the correct definition of truth, and so is this also not surmountable in causing and bringing about these declarations of war.

And yet if Mankind sets himself above God, and so therefore follows underneath his own influences of his own intelligence, is not his institutions somewhat flawed and proven unworthy of his governance of such institutions, then do not the children of Mankind also set themselves above the influences and presences of God, and yet who is the teacher and governor of such humanities, for is it not better to admit to ourselves that this is also the error of the way, and is this also not evenly unbalanced and less sustainable or prove worthy amongst us, as to whom shall be left to lead Mankind if he cannot lead Humanity himself, and yet beyond this, who has become the influencer of the influenced, and yet further still, if God has handed down if only one teaching of expression from one generation to another, then to whom shall it fall upon, and to what prevailing merit of distinction, as to whom from amongst us and those in our rankings beneath these stars of this material universe shall be found to be with such good promise, in bearing such good graces and blessings to be accorded and have set upon his being, if only to act and to perform such a profound role, as such a recipient with this bestowment upon himself, and yet further still, whom amongst us shall be found to be so willing if not highly regarded and noteworthy to become praiseworthy and respected and chosen as the first to be so honorably received in such a way with such invaluable revelations.

Even as Mankind marks out and sets out territories of distinction and borders, and also separates and divides the four corners of the Earth, it is also proven and noteworthy in saying, that God also does not mark out or set out territories, as God also makes no distinction between distancing the nations, as it is also prove worthy in itself to be, that God does not separate or divide the four corners of the Earth, as God throughout time had proven to Mankind and also unto Humanity, that the Earth from its' origins is God's creation in its entirety, and so therefore God is balanced and yet evenly impartial, and also apparently absent from such measures of inadmissible referencing, as it is upon our own interpretations of what is God's decrees unto Mankind in his lessons towards Humanity, and yet if Mankind makes a world, then is it not made for the whole of Humanity.

And so who is it that issues forth and grants Mankind authority over division, and yet upon its establishment, why does Mankind seek to undermine his own authority in blaming God, when found to be seeking such authority, especially when it is integral to his own greatest of beliefs, and endeavors, and life's purposes for Mankind unto Humanity, and yet we have that he has taught and deemed and seen himself unfit to ignore the fundamental principles and teaching blocks of truth, that even unto time immemorial has set him free from such burdens, as for this example to be extended to Humanity, if two men go out into the world in search of God, and yet one follows the mind, and the other follows the heart, and yet both are placed and set upon the path of journeying forth until they come a place of no understanding, then so shall it be that until the heart and the mind are reconciled, and unified in their complete understanding of one another, only then can God appear between them, as only then, can they hope and attempt to cooperate and communicate in coming to terms with uncovering and discovering the root of the truth concerning God.

But what is this truth surrounding God, is not God all things knowingly to all the people of all the nations, except that in as many ways and in as many guises, God is manifest in the heart and mind unto the whole of creation and within all the manifestations of all life, and so therefore Mankind must insist upon raising his own awareness in the consciousness that is God which is both the foundation and yet the principled pinnacle of what Humanity is and will be considered to become in the ages that proceed over time, as God is also influencing and guiding and preparing the way for all the peoples of all the nations, and in as many ways and in as many guises, so that Humanity can be fashioned and adorned and lifted and raised up within the consciousness of that part of God which is in himself, and yet so as to distinguish and to make what is unclear and yet unmatched and unparalleled to Mankind, is the simple truth, that one need may differ from the other, and yet all needs are met with accordingly, and yet one place upon the Earth may differ from the other, and yet all places are inhabited by God's creation, and yet one language and dialect may differ from the other, and yet all origins can become traced within the ancestry and the lineage in the history of civilization, as the truth of God is taught through Mankind's lessons unto and towards Humanity, which is in itself a story of huge and importance and proportions, as it is also the story of unlimited never endings, from the primal origins of the primordial universe, established by the presences of God amongst the primordial sentient beings, in that even as we, the destined recipients of the future of our beginning, are also the creation of the creator.

For the truth also concerning God, is also the distance taken between you and I, as in saying that God is not only the sustainer of light, but is also the constructer of matter, as God is also cloaked within all the mannerisms of the universal elements, as even we, when we are brought into that light, that so too do we, become cloaked in all mannerisms that are attributed to us through God, as over time, we are born and nurtured, and upon our maturing, we are natured and fashioned by our every changing environment, and yet even we in our maturing and ageing, are also given over to old age and frailty, and yet in coming to terms with our inevitable decaying and dying and eventual death, that still we are connected and affected by all the momentous occasions and events of our lives, as we are also within the full experience and wisdom, and yet still it is that with all mannerisms of elemental truths that we are revealed through to the light of our lives, and given over unto our fulfillment, and upon our reflections and connections to God.

And so for us to go into the presences of the world once again, then has not God requested it, that one of us should be granted leave to remain, and yet will it not burden and meet us with all the greatest demands of all sorrows, for if we should once again become separated from one another for even an instant, as our entire legacy is tied up and bound together as one, and so we must consider the verity of this sanction, and yet in both deciding and choosing who shall remain and stay without us, then at least let us first see who is willing to act as an advocate and volunteer in support of these promises of deliverance, and yet before the wheels of the Ophanim have begun to throw us all into the chaos of such innumerable numbers of accountancy's, then let me, Haven the Herald Angel stay and remain here as a beacon of hope and light, and forever dwell with for wherever it may needed to be extended too, for I have seen much and learnt much beyond my years of this Angeldom, but permit me this, that in the future that follows after you all, that you will remember to recollect me, as the Herald Angel of the Hosts of Heaven, and I shall be satisfied to stay and contend here amongst the Archangels and also to become settled and content enough with God and my Right Dieu et mon droit.

Authors Notes

It is of the utmost importance that we do not destroy any persons
personal faith, no matter what or how profoundly they may aspire
to be inspired to believe in something quite supernaturally or
unfathomable, so please consider this and find it in your heart to
know that faith is in the expression of living a life of piety and filled
with a magnitude of love, as some of us put our faith in people as
much as each other, as much as people put their faith in God or
Angels or Spirits or Science, so I only say this, that with faith, it is
only an attempt and a positive attitude that we are affirmed and just,
in believing that the narratives that we are all aiming to pursue and
fulfill and uncover, is to be accordingly just and right and true in our
pursuits in this life, as such is the faith, that I have in all of you.

The Angel Babies Story for me, was very much written and inspired
by many feelings of expression, that was buried very deeply inside
of me, as it was through my own exchanges, and relationships, and
journeying, and upon the discovery of both negative and positive
experiences, that often challenged my own beliefs, and personal
expectations of what I thought or felt was my own life's purpose, and
reason for being and doing, and very much what any one of us would
expect to be the result, or the outcome of their own personal life
choices based upon the status quo of our own design or choosing.

The story within itself, very much maintains its own conception
of intercession from one person to another, as we can only contain
the comprehension of the things that we most relate too, and that
which most commonly resembles and reflect our own emotions
and experiences, by tying in with something tangible that either
connects, or resonate at will deeply within us, as many of us have

the ability and intuit nature, to grasp things not merely as they are presented to us, but how things can also unfold and manifest in us, that are sometimes far beyond our everyday imaginings, and that are also equally hard to grasp and somewhat difficult to comprehend and let alone explain.

As we often learn to see such challenges and difficulties as these, especially in young minds, that react in responsive ways and are also equally gifted, or equally find it in themselves in life changing circumstances, to deal with prevailing situations, that most of us would take for granted, and would naturally see as the average norm, as we are all somewhat uniquely adjusted to deal with the same prevailing situation very differently, or even more so to uniquely perceive it in very different ways.

As for the question of how we all independently learn to communicate through these various means of creative, or artistic, or spiritual measures, is also simply a way of communicating to God as in prayer, as well as with one another, as all aspects are one of the same creation, as to whether such forms of expression can personify, or act as an intermediate medium, or channel to God, or indeed from one person to another, is again very much dependent upon the nature of its composition and expression, and the root from which it extends, and so for us to believe that our forbearers, or indeed our ancestors have the ability to intercede for us in such spiritual terms upon this our journey through life, is very much to say, that it is through their life's experiences, that we have become equipped, and given a wealth, and a portion of their life's history, with which for us to make our own individual efforts and choices, for us to be sure and certain of the way, in which we shall eventually come to be.

When we take a leap of faith, it is often into the unknown, and it is often associated with, or stems from the result of our constant fate being applied and presented to us in the context of a fear or phobia, insomuch so, that we must somehow, or at least come face to face with, or deal with, or come to terms with these matters arising, that are usually our own personal concerns, or worries, or anxieties toward a balanced or foreseeable reality, which is often beyond our immediate control, in that we are attempting to define and deal with this systematic physical, and spiritual progression, in the hope and the faith that we can resolve these personal matters, so as to allow us to put the mind and the heart at ease and to rest.

As it is often through our rationalizing, and our affirmation, and our professing or living with our beliefs, that what we often call, or come to terms with through our acceptance, is that through faith, belief and worship in God, that such personal matters, can easily be addressed, and dealt with, so as to overcome when facing such difficult and challenging obstacles, as even when in response to a negative impact that can have a harmful effect upon our physical bodies and being, we also often rely upon this same faith in the physical terms of our living and well being to guide us, and especially where we are often engaged in rationalizing with this phenomena, in the context of our faith, hope and belief, which often requires and demands us to look upon the world in a completely different way, so that we can reach far beyond the rational expectations of our own reality, and perceive to look forward into that of our metaphysical world.

As it is through this metaphysical world of all irrationality, and chaos and confusion, that a leap of faith is required to pass through and beyond the unknown context of our rational and conscious reality, and thus so as far as we can see, to understand our consciousness, as we believe it should be, in that we are contained in every aspect of our faith, hope and belief, as we are often presented with more than just a rational imagination, of what lies beyond our eventful fate or worries and concerns, and so within the mind of dreams, we are presented with a super imagination, where extraordinary things exist and take effect much beyond our physical comprehension, although very much aligned to the interconnectedness within our emotions, that brings with it a super reality, where we can accept the tangibility of these dreams upon realizing them, so as to be found and understood, as when we are found to be waking up in our day to day reality and activity, but also in choosing not to deny or extinguish these dreams as mere dreams, but to accept, and to see them, or refer to them as signs.

As of when we see such tell tale signs, or such premonitions forgoing, or foreboding us in our fate, it is very much that these signs often impact the most upon that of our conscious minds, as they are very much presented to us in an informative and abstract way, very much like a picture puzzle that we are busily attempting to piece together and work out, and very much in the way that we are attempting to put the heart and the mind at ease and to rest, so as to secure peace of mind in order to find and establish and maintain inner peace, as such signs as these, are often the ones that I am referring too, and can often and easily be presented to us in many ways, but to be sure and certain, if they are Godly or Divining messages upon intuition and translation, very much depends and largely relies upon us as individuals, as to what we are naturally engaged in and pursuing, in the same hope and light of the context, of this experience of such a Godly nature.

As such experiences are crucial and key, as to how we deal with any or all relationships, especially when we are developing a relationship within the Godly aspects of our lives, as more often than not, when we use such phrases and metaphors as, 'Going through a Door' or 'Crossing a Bridge, it is simply by saying such statements as these, or putting things in this way or context, that we decidedly know and acknowledge that a big change is about to occur, and develop or happen to us, and so we in ourselves are becoming equipped and prepared to deal with such changes, as they shall determine what shall be the eventual outcome of our fate, as there may already have been so many foretelling signs, much before the final impact or infinite sign is presented to us, insomuch so, that it may have already been subtly presented to us, much before the true perspective or picture of our reality has come to fruition and presented to us as a whole.

The whole being, is that which pieces itself together, with all the necessary facets and aspects of our Human Nature, Personality, Mannerisms and Characteristics and Traits, as all in all, it presents to us a vision, which sets us apart from one another, but also equally ties us all together in the event and act of completing our picture and journey through life, and it is through these instincts that we all naturally possess, and is all that is inextricably woven into the metaphysical fabric and the spiritual aspects of the heart and mind, and of those that are channeled along the lines of the minds meridians, and the intricate channels that give way to apprehensible intuitive mental awareness of signs and dreams, and or premonitions or visions, of how, or what we may choose to accept, or to objectively analyze, or to take note of and perceive in communication, or indeed how God may choose to communicate with or through us.

As it is in our realizing that within our personal fate and decisiveness, that we are calling upon, and facing a reality, that questions and presents itself to us all, as something that is profoundly spiritual and ambiguous, in relation to what we are all intrinsically held and bound by within our faith and beliefs, in that what we expect is about to unravel itself before us, as we begin to discover all that in which we are, as such is the expectation and the realization in our phobias and fears, that we may begin to readdress or even regress, or desist in such a course of action concerning these doubts and deliberations, so as not to offset or to promote any ideas that may bring about any personal demise, or disharmony, or disunity, that may trigger any negative aspectual forecasts or emotions within ourselves, as it is such a self fulfilling reality, that we are all in subjection too, in creating along and upon our own individual paths of merits and natural progression, that naturally such phenomena is presented and revealed to us as a whole, and is often profoundly real and yet maintains its simplicity, and is quite ordinarily so upon our realization of it, as if by mere chance that somehow deep down we already knew, that when we became aware of it, we somehow knew it to be so.

As it is these lessons in life, that are to be learnt from such self affirming challenges, so as to test our minds imagination and of course that which is at the very heart, of how we in our Human nature, can so easily push our abilities far beyond the boundaries, upon the premise of what is, or what is not possible, which brings to mind the verse and saying of the scripture and that is to say, that if anyone adds or takes away from this book, then so too shall their part be added or taken away, and yet if we continue further along this point, it also goes on to ask, who is worthy to remove this seal, so as to reveal the dream or the foreknowledge that we may all come to terms with our natural agreement and acceptance of it, as it is in knowing and accepting what shall befall us in our fate, as to what choice of action we must or can take, as such are the phobias and fears of trepidation that also gives way to the rise of hope, so that we may come face to face with destiny.

As with each new day comes a new beginning, and with each new beginning comes new hopes and new expectations, as there are also new obstacles and challenges to overcome, as such is the dawning of life, to present to us all, such necessary and redeemable qualities within the observations of our lives, for to have hope, is to look up toward the heavens, and to quietly and silently know, that within this observation, that the sky or indeed the heavens, are still upheld by the forces of nature, that govern from above albeit much to our amazement and expectations, and that life is ordinarily and justly so, as we in our appreciation cannot always see beyond that which is so perfectly bound and set in motion with us in this universe, as we simply learn to believe and accept that this is the way of our living and all things besides us, as we are within all that has become created and laid out before us.

And yet with this new day dawning, if not for us to simply wake up and to use our hopes, and our aspirations to ascend beyond the obvious point of creation, and to apply our spiritual nature and positive will of motivation toward it, and it toward us upon reflection, as in our overcoming and prevailing, within its and our own destiny and deliverance, as such is also our descent to take warmth and courage, and comfort and refuge, when we lay down to take rest and sleep beneath the Moon and the Stars above, is also to take strength and peace of mind, in the hope and the understanding that a new day beginning, and a new dawning shall be presented to us once again, as this is the way of the life that we have come to know it, within our own divine ability and acceptance of it.

As much as life is and can very much be a challenge, it also appears to state, that there is a thread of universal commonality running through the whole of creation no matter what we profess to live and abide by as human beings, as for me the basis of these requirements that extend from this commonality is food, shelter, clothing, companionship, and a sense of connection or clarity derived from self awareness, that is not to say that there is not much more for broad scope beyond this basic measure and requirement that puts us all on an equal footing with one another, no matter where we inhabit or dwell in the world.

And so what and where are we permitted upon this universal basis, to gravitate towards, or indeed to excel to, in order to fulfill our existential experiences and engage with our full potential, as many of us in our progression towards modernity, would indeed interpretate this kind of idea or philosophy, depending upon which part of the world we lived in or inhabited, as being very much viewed differently realized upon that same broad basis, which also brings me to ask, and to question, and to examine this brave new world within this context, or indeed as some would profess to say or mention, within this new world order, or new world system, as there is much to address and to consider for all concerned.

For once we have evolved and grown and matured away from our basic needs and requirements, it would also appear that many of us who have indeed excelled, or concluded in the context of a post-modernistic era of environment or society, to have almost achieved something, which is of a value, or at least on a par with something that is equally attributed, to that of a spiritual level of attainment, or indeed enlightenment, but when we address the cost of such achievement, we also begin to see that we are still somewhat grounded in our best efforts by this basic requirement, which is to achieve, acquire, and survive at will, and to endure, and to live, and to abide by such new discoveries of achievements.

As even in this progress and achievement of what we would wish, or presume to call a new world, how do we fairly address or balance, or differentiate between those of us who are yet to grasp the basis of this understanding that is required for us to excel, or indeed for us to fly, or indeed to reach the highest spiritual level of attainment of understanding, of being, doing, and knowing, as in realizing that indeed not many of us could have, or would have had the opportunity, or indeed the privilege, of exercising such expressions of freedom in our new found world.

As some of us are fundamentally held by the very conventions of what is required upon this, a basic level of our independence, maintenance, and survival, to regulate and maintain the simplicity of ourselves, and yet once we have experienced and entertained this new idea inside such a concept, our first response is how should we, or what should we do in order to engage with one another, to bring about its universality as a basic principle and as a must for all concerned, and how can it be any good for us, if indeed we all profoundly have separate agendas, or different ideals, as to what should, or could take precedence over the basic and fundamental needs to live out our lives, when food, and shelter, and clothing, and companionship, and a sense of self, or a clarity of awareness is needed at the very heart of what it is, to not only be, but remain humane.

As for the background, or indeed the backdrop, and the combining and dedicated efforts, that it has taken me as a writer to come to arrive at within this story of the Angel Babies, and of course the time that it has taken for me, to construct, and to collate the necessary, and if I may say worthy and worthwhile aspects, for this particular body of work to become written and completed within the trilogy of the Angel Babies, I would very much like just like to inform the readership, that upon exploration and construction of this body of work, that I myself as a person, have experienced several variables of conversions upon my spiritual and emotional being, upon the instruction and initiation of bringing the series of these books into the light.

For had I not been introduced into the many schools of thought and allied faiths of Christianity, Islam, Hare Krsna, Hindu, Buddhism, Dao and Shinto, that it may never have transpired or surmounted, or indeed would have been very much an arduous and challenging task, to find the right motivation for the narrative, very much needed and applied, with which to find and devise the relative inspiration, and ideas explored and written within the context and narrative of the characters and the storyline that I have presented to you as an author.

~ *Clive Alando Taylor*

Printed in the United States
By Bookmasters